This book belongs to:

....

Note to parents and carers

Read it yourself is a series of classic, traditional tales, written in a simple way to give children a confident and successful start to reading.

Each book is carefully structured to include many high-frequency words that are vital for first reading. The sentences on each page are supported closely by pictures to help with reading, and to offer lively details to talk about.

The books are graded into four levels that progressively introduce wider vocabulary and longer stories as a reader's ability grows.

Ideas for use

- Begin by looking through the book and talking about the pictures. Has your child heard this story before?

- Help her with any words she does not know, either by helping her to sound them out or supplying them yourself.

- Developing readers can be concentrating so hard on the words that they sometimes don't fully grasp the meaning of what they're reading. Answering the puzzle questions on pages 30 and 31 will help with understanding.

For more information and advice, visit www.ladybird.com/readityourself

Level 2 is ideal for children who have received some reading instruction and can read short, simple sentences with help.

Special features:

Frequent repetition of main story words and phrases

Short, simple sentences

The first little pig built his house of straw.

The second little pig built his house of sticks.

The third little pig built his house of bricks.

Large, clear type

"Then I'll huff and I'll puff and I'll blow your house down," said the big, bad wolf.

And he huffed and he puffed and he blew the house down!

Careful match between story and pictures

15

Educational Consultant: Geraldine Taylor

A catalogue record for this book is available from the British Library

Published by Ladybird Books Ltd
80 Strand, London, WC2R 0RL
A Penguin Company

2 4 6 8 10 9 7 5 3
© LADYBIRD BOOKS LTD MMX
Ladybird, Read It Yourself and the Ladybird Logo are registered or
unregistered trade marks of Ladybird Books Limited.

ISBN: 978-1-40930-363-3

Printed in China

The
Three Little Pigs

Illustrated by Virginia Allyn

Once upon a time,
there were three little pigs.

One day, they went out
to build their own houses.

The first little pig built his house of straw.

The second little pig built his house of sticks.

The third little pig built his house of bricks.

Along came a big, bad wolf. He went up to the house of straw.

"Little pig, little pig, let me come in," said the big, bad wolf.

But the first little pig said, "By the hair of my chinny, chin, chin, I will not let you in!"

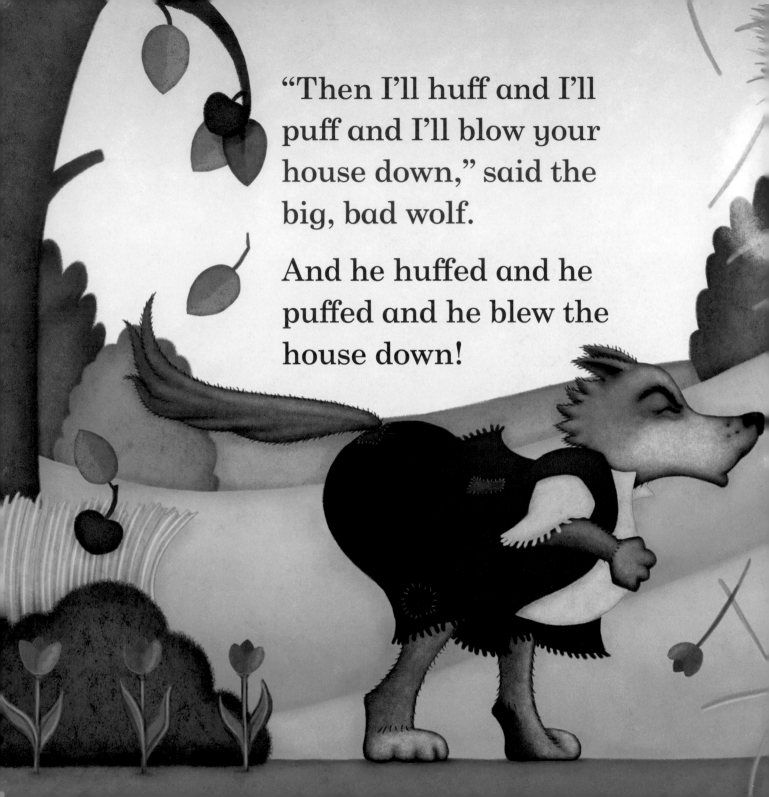

"Then I'll huff and I'll puff and I'll blow your house down," said the big, bad wolf.

And he huffed and he puffed and he blew the house down!

The big, bad wolf went up
to the house of sticks.

"Little pig, little pig,
let me come in," he said.

But the second little pig said, "By the hair of my chinny, chin, chin, I will not let you in!"

"Then I'll huff and I'll puff and I'll blow your house down," said the big, bad wolf.

And he huffed and he puffed and he blew the house down!

The big, bad wolf went up
to the house of bricks.

"Little pig, little pig,
let me come in," he said.

But the third little pig said, "By the hair of my chinny, chin, chin, I will not let you in!"

"Then I'll huff and I'll puff and I'll blow your house down," said the big, bad wolf.

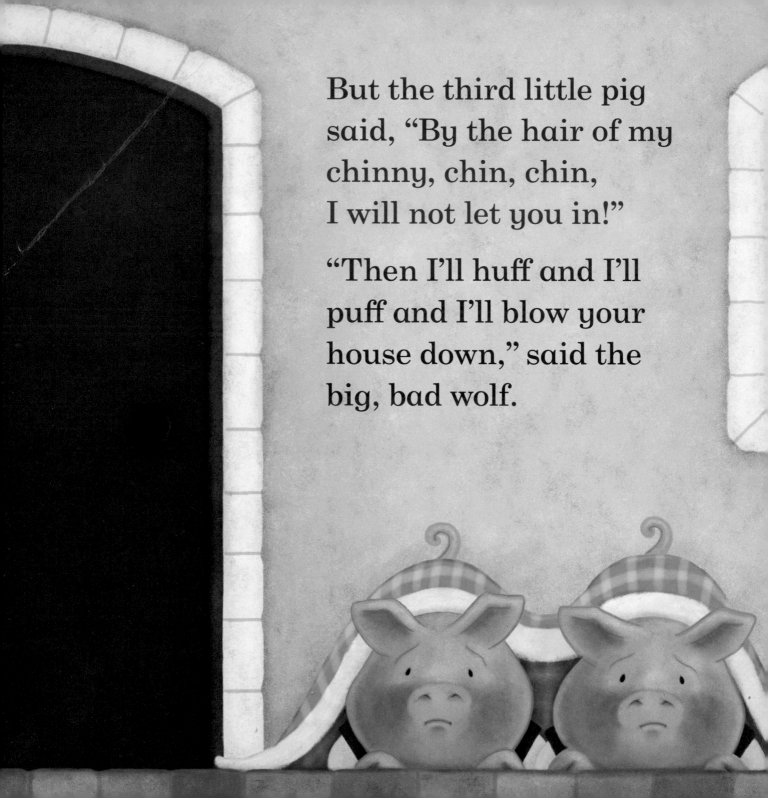

So he huffed and he puffed and he huffed and he puffed, but he could not blow the house down.

The big, bad wolf climbed on top of the house and came down the chimney...

Splash!

And that was the end of the big, bad wolf.

29

How much do you remember about the story of The Three Little Pigs? Answer these questions and find out!

- What is the first little pig's house made of?

- What do the three little pigs say to the big, bad wolf when he wants to come in?

- What happens when the big, bad wolf tries to blow down the house of bricks?

- How do the three little pigs trick the big, bad wolf?

Look at the pictures and match the pigs to their houses. Can you spot the big, bad wolf?

sticks

straw

bricks 31

Read it yourself
with Ladybird

The Three Billy Goats Gruff

Cinderella

Little Red Hen

Goldilocks and the Three Bears

The Magic Porridge Pot

The Ugly Duckling

The Gingerbread Man

Sleeping Beauty

Sly Fox and Red Hen

The Three Little Pigs

Town Mouse and Country Mouse

Little Red Riding Hood

The Elves and the Shoemaker

Jack and the Beanstalk

The Pied Piper of Hamelin

The Wizard of Oz

Collect all the titles in the series.